'Jason wandered down the beach [...] pool.

"Crab," he called gently.

There was no movement.

"Crab."

Still nothing.

"Crab!" He stared down into the water. It was quite clear and there was absolutely no sign of him at all. Where was he? "Crab?" He shifted rocks, debris, seaweed, urchins, anemones, but the crab wasn't there . . . '

To Jason, the big crab that lives in a rock pool near his home on the run-down old pier, is a good-luck charm, a talisman. And Jason needs all the luck Crab can give when the horrible Atkins family arrive and Jason is caught up in a mystery — a mystery that is to lead him into a dangerous adventure!

Also available by Anthony Masters,
and published by Yearling Books:

FROG

CRAB

CRAB

ANTHONY MASTERS

YEARLING BOOKS

CRAB

A YEARLING BOOK 0 440 86285 X

First publication in Great Britain

PRINTING HISTORY

Yearling edition published 1992
Yearling edition reprinted 1992

This book is set in 14/16pt Century Schoolbook by
Chippendale Type Ltd., Otley, West Yorkshire.

Yearling Books are published by Transworld Publishers Ltd.,
61–63 Uxbridge Road, Ealing, London W5 5SA, in Australia by
Transworld Publishers (Australia) Pty. Ltd., 15–23 Helles
Avenue, Moorebank, NSW 2170, and in New Zealand by
Transworld Publishers (N.Z.) Ltd., 3 William Pickering
Drive, Albany, Auckland.

Printed and bound in Great Britain by
Cox & Wyman Ltd., Reading, Berks.

To Gill Bromley and Maggi Waite, innovative children's librarians, with my love and admiration. Also to all my friends in the Hastings Writers' Group.

CHAPTER ONE

'Just what do you think you're doing?'

Adam Atkins looked up from the rock pool, his thin, townie face squinting up at Jason in a mixture of anger and suspicion. He had a stick in his hand and was poking about, stirring up the grey-green water until it clouded over.

'Just having a look.'

'You're not. You're bullying Crab.' Jason Segal was tousle-haired and stockily built, bigger than Adam but not as streetwise.

'Crab? What do you mean, "Crab"?'

'He's big and he lives in this pool – always has done. I've known him for a long time.'

Adam laughed raucously. 'Pal of yours, is he?'

'Yes, and you leave him alone.'

Adam stirred the water again and Jason advanced threateningly.

'Get that stick out of the pool.'

'Push off!'

'Get it out – now!'

'You gonna make me?' Adam stood

10

up. He was small but muscular, and Jason saw there was a hungry look in his eyes that he had seen in a few other boys before; it was a look that meant they liked fighting. Could he beat him? Jason wondered. He just didn't know.

'Yes, I'll make you,' said Jason as calmly as he could.

Immediately Adam dropped the stick and put up his fists.

'Oi!' They were circling each other as Sam Segal, Jason's father, yelled from the pier. 'What do you two think you're doing?'

'Only play-fighting, Mr Segal,' said Adam, backing off and trying to grin.

'Doesn't look like it to me.' Sam Segal was an enormous man, almost as wide as he was tall, with a great bushy beard and large matted eye-brows. He had once been a showman, travelling in fairs up and down the country with his rides. Now he had settled down, and over the last couple of years had leased the run-down old pier in the south-coast town of Portsea and opened Segal's Super Sensation – an amusement centre that included a hall of mirrors, a fortune-teller's booth, slot machines, a scruffy tea-room, a bingo parlour and a rifle range. It wasn't much of a place, but Sam was very proud of it and had ambitious plans for expansion. Just now he was looking fierce and dis-appointed as he strode off the pier and scrunched over the shingle beach. 'I thought you two were meant to be trying to hit it off.'

'Yes, Dad.'

'Yes, Mr Segal.'

'So far you *are* hitting it off – literally.'

'It was a game, Mr Segal,' whined Adam. 'Wasn't it, Jason?'

'Yes, it was a game,' Jason said reluctantly.

Sam looked at them both sus-piciously. Adam Atkins was the son of Eileen and Arthur Atkins whom he had hired to help out on the pier so that he could have more time to develop a dodgem track while his wife Winnie set about planning a big slide. Gran, Sam's mother, helped keep house. She was a retired fortune-teller, and although she had given up her professional name of Vera the Visionary, some of her cronies still came round to tea, wanting to know what the future held for them, and they would gather round the cups like ancient vultures.

Eileen Atkins claimed to be an astrologer, palmist and clairvoyant and, much to Gran's disgust, had opened up the old booth, using *her* professional name of Madame Zorza. Sam had let them have some rooms at the back of the bingo hall as temporary accommodation, but Jason was sorry they had come; he just didn't like the family. There was something greedy and shifty about Eileen, and Arthur had a sinister air about him as if he would stop at nothing to get his own way. Somehow

Jason had the curious feeling that Arthur had some kind of hold over his dad. He was often quite rude to him – as if *he* was the boss – and he seemed to get away with it. Once Jason had asked his dad if he had known Arthur in the past and, although he was quickly told to 'mind his own business', Jason was quite certain that his father looked worried. Adam, however tough he pretended to be, was definitely afraid of his father. Jason had noticed that Adam often had the odd bruise, and had once had a black eye. But when Jason had pointed it out to his dad, Sam – who was usually so kind – had just said that it was nothing to do with them.

'Come on then, Adam,' said Sam. 'Your dad wants you to give me a hand clearing up the bingo hall for tonight.'

Grumbling, Adam did as he was told, but not without giving Jason a mocking backward glance.

'Go on – push off,' whispered Jason.

'I'll flatten you,' was Adam's parting shot.

He ran off across the pebbles to the ramp that led up to the pier. It was quite small, a long, thin arm stretching out into the sea, and had a turnstile and a box office with a big garish sign hanging over it bearing the notice 'Segal's Super Sensation'. There was a large domed hall which connected with a smaller one that was now the bingo parlour. A long windswept walkway covered by a wooden canopy ran all around, and there was a tea-room and then a wide, circular strip of decking where they were planning to put the dodgems and the slide. At the very end of the pier, on a lower platform, dozens of fishermen sat, immobile as dolls until they made the occasional cast, staring out at the golden September sea.

Once Adam had gone, Jason knelt down by the pool and began to peer

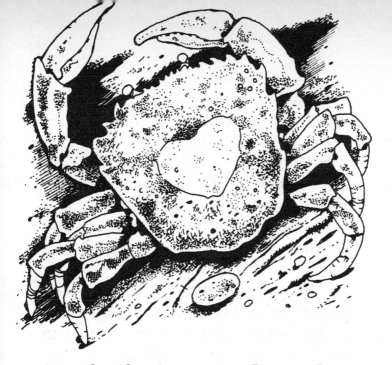

into the clearing water. It was deep
and dark and cold, but he could see
Crab at the bottom, gently moving
his pincers, his stalk eyes staring up
at him with interest. He had one very
distinctive marking on his shell which
looked like a heart – or at least Jason
felt it did. Well, he's all right, thought
Jason, but he'd have to keep an eye
on Adam.

He heard the crunch of his dad's
boots on the pebbles and looked up.

'How's Crab?' asked his father.

'He's OK. I don't trust Adam with him though. I'm scared he'll hurt him – you know what he's like.'

Sam nodded. He knew how fond Jason was of Crab and he never mocked his only child's affection – however strange it was.

'That Adam – he needs a good hiding,' observed Sam.

'And I'll give it to him, Dad,' said Jason without conviction.

'No, I don't want trouble. I reckon his father'll take care of that.'

'He's horrible,' Jason burst out.

'I've got to have the staff,' replied Sam. His voice was apologetic, but Jason was sure that he was hiding something. 'They're hard to come by,' he added too quickly.

'Yeah.'

'But we'll have to keep them in line, won't we, son?'

Jason nodded. 'If he hurts Crab, I'll kill him.'

'That makes two of us,' reassured his father.

*

Jason had noticed something very odd about Eileen and Arthur Atkins. For one thing they seemed to have a good number of visitors, and they were all rough-looking men who would usually arrive after dark, stay for half an hour and go away again. They came in twos and threes and usually saw Arthur. Eileen invariably came out and tidied up her booth very briskly, as if she had been given something to do which she resented. Jason had asked his father about the visitors and Sam had told him that Arthur Atkins was a part-time bookmaker, but Jason wasn't so sure; Eileen always seemed so bad-tempered when they came, as if she was being left out of something more interesting than a small bookmaking business. She was an extraordinary-looking woman: tall and dramatic, with black hair and a heavily made-up face with a long beaky nose and flashing haughty eyes. Eileen Atkins spoke in a fearfully grand way, with many sweeping gestures, and was a complete contrast to her sly husband who was a weaselly little man with a long walrus moustache, a completely bald head that looked like a lump of suet, and eyes that always seemed to be very cold. Gran said the Atkins had done the same work on some other piers, but they hadn't lasted very long in any of their previous jobs.

'Coming in for tea?' asked Sam.

'OK, Dad.'

They walked slowly to the ramp. It was a weekday, school was back and the season was coming to an end. There weren't very many punters today but it had been a good summer. Sam looked up at the sign over the pier and then smiled at his son affectionately. 'All this will be yours one day, if you want it, Jason.'

'Great, Dad.' Jason loved his father in these expansive moods.

' 'Course, it's nothing now. But

when I get them dodgems sorted and your mum's fixed the slide with the builders, well, the sky's the limit. I've got room to expand and I'll have a classy restaurant – maybe a disco.'

They wandered through the turnstile, nodding at Alfie, the old retired fisherman who took the money, and walked on past the bingo hall and amusements towards the tea-room. A few punters were playing the machines, and Jason's heart swelled with pride as it often did when he walked with his dad on the pier.

CHAPTER TWO

'You're late.'

Winnie Segal, Jason's mum, brought them back to earth with a bump as she stood at the door of the tea-room. She was a practical woman, determined that her husband's ambitions for the run-down old pier should succeed. But Jason had noticed that over the last few weeks she had been getting more and more tired, and there was something in her eyes that told him she was really feeling the strain. Now, however, she smiled at them both affectionately and just told them to hurry upstairs for their tea.

The Segals had a flat over the building, cool in the summer and cosy, if storm-lashed, in the winter. It was like living on a ship, and Jason loved the feeling of the elements being all around them, battering at his bedroom window. When the weather was very bad, he would often think of Crab, motionless at the bottom of his pool, staring up at its rippled, wind tossed surface. He was a mysterious creature with the heart shape on his shell, and for some reason Jason couldn't really understand, he felt a great kinship with him. He had been there ever since the Segals had moved on to the pier five years ago and, to Jason, Crab was a kind of good-luck charm.

Although Jason's parents were indulgent about Crab, only his gran realized how important he was to him. Maybe it was because he was an only child and didn't have too many other children to play with, particularly as he was always busy working on the pier, or maybe it was because

Jason was worried about the pressure that always seemed to be on his parents. Either way, Crab was someone to be alone with, and often Gran would come and sit with Jason, knitting silently or telling him about her old fortune-telling days. She didn't seem to mind the weather and Jason was glad to have her company. He also hoped Crab liked her too.

A few weeks ago, Jason had told Gran how much he hated Adam and how he didn't think they could avoid a fight much longer. She had nodded, her head bent over a copy of the *Sun*, but although she didn't look up, he knew that she had been listening and would say something when she was ready. At length she had asked, 'Are you frightened he'll harm Crab?'

'Yeah, he's really got it in for him. Why should he hate Crab so much? I have to watch him all the time.'

'I suppose Adam reckons he's got nothing – and you've got everything. Mum and Dad and me and Crab. He

24

knows how much you love Crab, and
he can't hurt the grown-ups so he
tries to hurt you. Don't you see?'

'He's got his mum and dad.'

'Some mum and dad. I used to
know Eileen years ago. She's a
right—'

'Did you know Arthur?' Jason had
asked. He had never really heard her
talk about the Atkins before.

'No—' she had said slowly. 'I never
knew Arthur, and thank God for
that. I don't want to know him now.
He's a nasty bit of work. More than
that – he's evil, he is.'

'Wish Dad would get rid of him,'
Jason had muttered.

Gran had been silent, as if she was
holding something back. Then she
had started to say something and had
stopped abruptly.

'What's up, Gran?'

'Nothing.'

'You sure?'

'I said – nothing.' She had been
quite snappy. Then she had added
hurriedly, "Course, he knocks him

around. We all know that. It's not fair – he's only a kid.'

'Maybe he deserves it,' Jason had said unsympathetically.

'No, he doesn't deserve it. That's why he's the way he is.'

The phrase rang in Jason's mind as he walked into the kitchen. He often thought about what Gran had said, but it still didn't make him feel any better about Adam. He hated him and knew he would try and harm Crab, so Jason was determined to be always on his guard.

'Atkins has got his punters again,' said Gran as she put down plates of sausages, chips and onions. 'Coming and going,' she muttered and hobbled back to the stove. Her crouched figure looked frail today, but she was tough and must have cooked thousands of fry-ups in her time.

'It's a sideline,' said Sam absently.

'And *she* was up here, asking if she could put up a stand selling dressed crab.' Winnie sniffed slightly, and Jason wondered once again why his parents didn't get rid of the Atkins. There was no doubt that neither his father nor mother could bear them, and yet they were employing them. Whenever he asked, Jason received some vague, inadequate, misleading reply so he had simply given up asking. Of course, he realized that to make any real money from the battered old pier they had to expand, and staff were hard to come by on the low wages the Segals were just able to pay.

'Eileen would like to do a dummy run now,' continued Winnie. 'Says she could use an old barrow.'

Gran snorted but said nothing.

Dressed crab, wondered Jason, suddenly feeling a twinge of anxiety. But she wouldn't go searching in rock pools, would she? Surely she'd get the crabs off the boats.

'But we're out of season – almost,' grumbled Sam, attacking his sausages.

'Says she wants to practise the dressing.'

'And she can cope with this as well as the fortune-telling?'

'That's what she says.'

'That woman will bring us no good – like her good-for-nothing husband,' muttered Gran. Jason noticed that Mum gave her a warning glance and then, seeing that Jason was watching, quickly looked away.

After tea, Jason wandered off to the park to kick a ball round with some of his mates. On his way back to their flat above the tea-room, he had to pass the bingo parlour and the Atkins' accommodation on the ground floor at the back. The lights were on, despite the fact that it was still daylight, and Jason was curious. He looked at his watch. Eight. He was late, but . . . Jason looked carefully around him. Nobody. No punters. Nothing. He would take a quick peep in at the Atkins' window.

A quick peep was enough. There

was no sign of Adam, but Eileen and Arthur were both sitting at the table under the light. Eileen's big dark eyes were shining, and Arthur, his suet head gleaming in the lamplight, was shuffling through a stack of paper. Then Jason realized it wasn't paper. Arthur Atkins was counting money — hundreds and hundreds of crisp, crackling bank notes — and on his lips was a most unpleasant smile.

CHAPTER THREE

Jason crouched by Crab's pool. He
knew he would have to go home soon
or he would be late for bed and his
mum would make a fuss, but he'd had
to go down to the pool to think. Why
were the Atkins counting so much
money? It was far more than any
bingo take could ever produce, so
where had it come from? And why?
Who did it belong to? The questions
raced around his mind in the darkness. He would have to tell his
parents. Then another thought came
to him. Could Arthur Atkins have

made all that money from his other job – from his takings as a bookie? Well, maybe. Jason felt a bit deflated; certainly this was the most likely explanation.

He glanced towards the pool and saw that Crab had hauled himself right out on to the beach and seemed to be staring up at the moon. What was he thinking? What secrets did he know? Jason pulled himself together. Crab was just an ordinary crab, despite his strange markings, and that was it. He might well feel like a good-luck charm to Jason – but that's all he was, he told himself firmly. And as for the Atkins, it must be bookie's money – and that was the end of the matter too.

He stood up, yawning and stretching. He'd better go in now or he'd really get it in the neck.

Jason usually slept very well without dreaming, but that night he tossed and turned while Crab clawed his way through a gathering nightmare of wild sea with his gran riding the breakers. Jason was marking time on the shoreline, and then, quite suddenly, he was pedalling a pedal boat, plunging up and over the swell. He kept reciting a poem, but he couldn't hear his own voice because of the crashing of the waves.

Then, out of a whirlpool, the head of a serpent appeared. There was something familiar about it, but Jason couldn't think what it was. Suddenly the serpent head was replaced by Eileen's, smiling in that superior way she had. Then she rose further up out of the swirling water and, to his horror, Jason saw that she was holding a plate of dressed crab. He could see the heart-shaped mark on part of the shell that was carefully displayed on a bed of lettuce.

'Here we are, Jason,' she said. 'A really tasty dish for you.' Eileen burst into screams of cackling witch-like laughter.

Jason shot bolt upright in bed. Something beyond the awful nightmare had woken him. He was sweating as he rose and went across to the window. From there, he could just see the shore, the bingo parlour and the ramp in the moonlight. Jason looked at his watch and saw that it was just after three in the morning. On the ramp, a van was being pushed towards the service road that led from the pier to the promenade. Heaving and sweating, Arthur Atkins was doing the pushing while his wife, Eileen, was sitting at the wheel. Had it broken down? Jason wondered. He would have to go and find out. He checked again and saw that the tide was out. If he crept out the back way, he could go under the pier on the sand and hide in the shadows. That way, he could probably overhear what they were saying.

Within seconds, Jason had scrambled out of his back window, on to the flat roof, down on to the boards of the pier and then down the flight of steps that had once been part of a jetty. He hit the flat, smooth sand softly and ran between the rusting, seaweed-hung columns until he was near the van that was still being pushed. Hiding himself as best he could, Jason strained to hear the hissed whispers. It wasn't difficult as the hissing was becoming sharper and more piercing. In fact, it was becoming very angry indeed.

'Listen,' whispered Eileen. 'I'm going to switch on the engine.'

'No!' Arthur was wearing a huge dressing-gown. He stopped pushing for a breather. 'You've already started this heap of junk and it sounded like a DC10. Trust Harry to lend me a wreck like this.'

'You sure that you got those special compartments bolted on safely?'

Arthur gave her a look of withering scorn.

'Just spent most of the night fixing 'em, haven't I?'

'I'm only checking.'

'No need to check on me,' he snarled. 'You get this clapped-out load of cobblers to Weston and then he can do the job.'

'What if the van folds up on him too?' she asked.

'He's a good mechanic. He'll sort it all out. You can rely on Weston. After all, he's taking a bigger cut than us.'

Eileen's voice was low and tense as she said, 'I don't want to have to deal with that Weston man again. There's something about him that – I don't know – makes me shudder. He's really dangerous, Arthur.'

'Listen—' he was impatient '—this isn't the time to get cold feet, Eileen. With our share we can pop off to sunny Spain and live like lords. All we're doing is sorting out a hidey-hole until the heat dies down. Right?'

'Can we trust him though?'

'Eileen! It's too late for all this. Let's get going.'

'All right,' she snapped. 'Get stuck

in and push.'

Arthur went to the back of the van and put his shoulder against the back door.

'Push, Arthur, push,' commanded Eileen.

'I am,' came the panting reply.

'Harder!'

He swore at her and tried again. But this time Arthur's feet slid away from him and he fell in a heap on the slippery, seaweed-encrusted road.

'What are you doing?' she whispered furiously.

'What do you think I'm doing?' spluttered Arthur, trying to scramble to his feet and ending up in the muck again.

The scene was becoming such a farce that Jason felt like giggling and only restrained himself with the utmost difficulty. Then he saw Arthur's face and suddenly the situation no longer seemed funny, for his eyes were blazing with barely controlled fury.

Arthur stopped pushing and straightened up. Then he turned again and heaved. Gradually the van jerked on to the promenade which ran slightly downhill. Gasping for breath, Arthur ran alongside the slowly moving vehicle.

'Don't start the engine until you're right down the end of the prom.'

'OK,' she replied crossly.

'I'll see you when you've passed the truck over to Weston.'

Eileen chuckled with sudden glee. 'We're going to make our fortunes over this.'

'Keep your voice down, woman.' Arthur gave her a really murderous look.

Eileen then drove away as quickly as she could, while Arthur crept back across the boards towards the bingo parlour. They were up to something all right, thought Jason. He had seen it with his own eyes now, and the only thing to do was to persuade his parents to believe him.

CHAPTER FOUR

Jason went back to bed and lay awake till a grey dawn came up over the tall wooden fishermen's drying sheds that stood next door to the pier. This part of the old town was the centre of the small fishing industry which still flourished in Portsea. The boats were drawn high up on the pebbles by winches, and the whole area was littered with fish boxes, machinery, old nets and little huts that formed a fish market. Usually Jason loved looking down at this compact little world and the *Morning*

Glory, the boat Dad jointly owned with one of the fishermen. He had taken Jason out several times on the tiny craft, making him realize how dangerous the sea could be and how hard it was to make a living out of fishing. Dad loved the *Morning Glory* but he'd been so preoccupied with Segal's Super Sensation recently that they hadn't been on an expedition together for ages.

This morning, however, Jason only had one burning thought on his mind: what he'd seen last night. Eventually he could bear it no longer. Looking at his watch he saw it was almost 5.30 a.m. Time to wake up his parents and tell them.

Jason knocked on their bedroom door. There was no answer so he knocked again. Eventually, his father's sleepy voice muttered, 'Was-samatter?'

'Dad.'

'Eh?'

'*Dad.*'

'Jason. What's the time?'

'It's early. I want to talk to you,' he whispered urgently.

'It had better be important,' said his dad fiercely. 'I'll never go back to sleep now.'

'It *is* important.'

'Come in then.'

They were both sitting up in bed, looking ready for an argument. Mum was yawning and rubbing her eyes. 'Jason lovey, what on earth's the matter?'

'The Atkins – they were pushing their van out last night.'

'So?' His dad gave the most enormous yawn.

'At three in the morning.'

'Something to do with the book-makers,' said Mum impatiently. 'He told us he had to send a van up to the racecourse at any hour of the night.'

'What for?' asked Jason suspiciously.

'Something to do with setting up a stand,' said Dad. 'You have to get

41

there early to bag your pitch or something.'

'But it was *three o'clock*.'

'They *said* any hour of the night,'
said Mum in a dangerously calm
voice. 'Is this *all* you've come to tell
us, Jason? Have you seen what the
time is?'

'Arthur pushed the van so it
wouldn't make a noise,' said Jason
insistently.

'That was considerate of him,' said
Dad.

'They didn't want to be heard.'
Jason was getting desperate.

'Of course they didn't.' Mum was
sarcastic. 'Eileen wouldn't want me
to lose my beauty sleep – unlike you.'

'Arthur's bolted on special compartments to the van,' gabbled Jason.

'Security I expect,' replied his dad.
'He probably carries a load of cash
around.'

'And they're talking about a man
called Weston doing the job and
he's taking a bigger cut and he's

dangerous and they're popping off to sunny Spain after they've sorted out a hidey-hole and they're making their fortunes and—' Jason paused, completely out of breath. He saw his dad exchange a warning glance with his mum.

'Look, son.' His father spoke very slowly, as if Jason was some kind of idiot. 'He's a bookmaker, all right? So he handles large sums of money. Right? The van's being used to pick it up. Right? And as for your hidey-holes and jobs and Spain and whatever else you said – it's all to do with his business.'

There was a long pause.

'Right?' his father said again.

'Right,' said Jason slowly. He didn't know what to think. Maybe he was completely wrong and had totally misinterpreted everything he had seen and heard.

'So you've made a mistake, haven't you?' said Mum. There was a note in her voice that he had never heard before. What was it? She sounded almost desperate, almost at breaking point.

'Maybe.'

'You made a mistake,' she persisted.

'Yes, Mum.'

'Look, son.' His father's voice was clipped, tense. 'I know you don't get on that well with Adam but you've got to try.'

'She's after Crab – that Eileen,' Jason blurted out. He had to make some kind of accusation, some kind of justification for it all.

'What?'

'She wants to catch him. Serve him up dressed.'

His dad laughed unfeelingly. 'What's he going to wear? A suit? Or something more casual?'

It wasn't fair. They were laughing at him now. Last night his father had been supportive about Crab; now he was just taking the mickey. Jason felt hot and angry tears pricking at the back of his eyes. Dad knew how much he loved Crab; he shouldn't be sending him up.

'Don't be rotten, Sam,' said his mother, coming to the rescue. 'Eileen wouldn't touch a crab in a pool; you never know where it might have been.'

'He's very clean,' sniffed Jason.

'I know, love. But she'd take crabs off the boats, wouldn't she?'

'S'pose so.'

'Now look—' Dad spoke slowly and deliberately '—I know Adam can be a bit of a pain, but without Eileen and Arthur I'd be stuck. We couldn't expand the business. Couldn't even run it. Do you get me?'

Jason heard a note of desperation in his father's voice too now, but he replied easily, not wanting to upset either of them any further, 'I get you.'

CHAPTER FIVE

Today was Saturday and there were quite a few visitors to the pier. Business was brisk and the amusement arcade, hall of mirrors, rifle range, bingo parlour and fortune-telling booth were doing well. Next to the booth was the dressed-crab stall. Eileen had worked hard all the early morning, buying and cooking, and now Adam was behind the counter, looking sharp and businesslike.

Over the weekends, Jason worked for his dad. He was very conscientious, and as a result received a good wage which he was saving to buy a mountain bike. Today he was painting the iron balustrades of the pier a brilliant white. The salt made them rust very quickly, and they needed repainting at least twice a year. The design was Victorian and full of fancy scroll work, so it was an intricate and rewarding job. Gradually Jason worked his way down towards Adam's stall. He felt exhausted after last night and he was still puzzled and horribly worried, not just as a result of what he had overheard, but by the way his parents had deliberately tried to cover everything up. Or had they? The situation spun round and round in his mind, making everything inextricably confused.

'Wotcher,' said Adam, smiling at him maliciously. Jason noticed a fresh bruise on his cheek, but he seemed as needle-sharp and as pushy as ever.

'Yeah.' Jason bent over his work, trying to avoid a conversation, but Adam was intent on talking to him.

'Like the crabs?'

'They're OK.'

'Mum's done 'em good.'

'Yeah.'

'Up early she was, looking round them rock pools.'

'Rock pools?'

'Well, they're nice and fresh down there.'

Jason straightened up. Was he winding him up? He must be.

'See.' Adam held up a crab. 'Recognize our old friend?'

Jason walked over to him. 'Your mum got those off the boats.'

'Most of 'em.' Adam had a swaggering look that wasn't very nice to watch.

'What do you mean?'

'Well, I got one or two for her.'

'What?' Jason was aghast.

'You heard.'

Jason stared at the crab. Was there something vaguely familiar about it? A wave of panic rose up inside him.

'Where did you get that?'

'Rock pool. Somewhere near.' Adam grinned wickedly.

'I'll be back.'

'Where're you going?'

'I *said* – I'll be back.' Jason sprinted off down the ramp and on to the beach. His heart was pounding. If he's touched him, I'll kill him, he promised himself over and over again.

Jason knelt down and looked into the pool, only to find there was nothing there. No Crab. He sat up and then jumped to his feet.

'Adam!' he yelled.

There was a wave from behind the crab stall, casual yet mocking.

'I'll get you,' Jason shouted, shaking his fist, the hot tears running down his face.

He knelt down again by the pool and stared despairingly into it. Then his heart leaped as he saw a slow movement and Crab came out from behind a stone, his body grey-green,

49

his eyes glowing, the heart-shaped mark clearly showing on his shell.

'Oh, Crab,' Jason sighed. 'Crab – you're safe.'

The little stalk eyes sparkled, and Jason's relief turned to anger again – Adam had deliberately wound him up and humiliated him. He would deal with him.

When Jason arrived back at the pier, he walked slowly over to the grinning Adam.

'Thought that was funny, did you?'

'Sort of.'

'Having a bit of a laugh?'

'Why not?'

'OK – here's another one.' Jason casually strolled over to his tin of paint and picked it up. Slowly he returned to the crab stall.

'What you doing with that?' asked Adam nervously.

'Not a lot.'

'Hang on—'

Jason slowly raised the tin and took aim. 'I thought I might improve the way you look.'

Adam lunged forward and tried to grab at the tin.

'Give you a new image,' Jason finished and hurled at least half a tin of white paint over Adam's head and shoulders. 'How's that then?'

Adam gave a terrible shriek as the white paint dripped down his face and all over his clothes. He looked like a bedraggled cross between a clown and a ghost.

'Mum!'

A small crowd began to gather.

'Mum!'

'What's up?' Eileen poked her head out of her booth. 'Can't you see I'm with a client?'

'Look what he's done!'

'Blimey!' Her ladylike air completely deserted her as she stared at her son. 'Who – did – that?'

'He did.'

'Jason?'

'Him!'

Eileen Atkins turned on Jason furiously. 'You did that, did you?' She was swathed in scarves and a shawl, despite the warm September afternoon. Meanwhile, an elderly man who was having his fortune told also appeared.

'Er, Madame Zorza – we were in the middle—'

'I'm so sorry, Mr Fawcett. There appears to have been something of a – er – an unfortunate – my son is covered in paint,' said Eileen, trying to control her fury.

'Oh dear.'

'Will you excuse me for ten minutes?'

'Of course.'

'Please sit in the booth and help yourself to a cup of tea.' The gracious smile disappeared from her face as she grabbed the least paint-covered part of the still howling Adam and dragged him off towards their flat. As the curious crowd parted, she snapped at Jason, 'You'll be for the high jump.'

'He told me you'd cooked Crab!'

'I don't care what he told you – you're for it.'

*

'Dad?'

'Yes, son?'

Jason walked slowly into the flat, knowing that he would have to tell his father everything. There was no way out, for soon the Atkins would be hotfooting it over, full of furious complaints. Anyway, the more he was open with his dad, the more his dad might be open with him. But Jason wasn't so sure of that. His dad had kept quiet for so long that it would take a lot to make him confide in him. But what, wondered Jason, was a lot? Could this be enough?

'Er.'

'Well?' His father looked at him suspiciously.

'I poured paint over Adam.'

'You did *what*?'

'I – I poured paint over Adam,' said Jason unhappily.

'You mean—'

'He's covered in paint. White paint.'

'Blimey.'

'Yeah.'

There was a long silence. Then Sam said slowly, 'What about the Atkins?'

'Eileen's not very pleased.'

Sam winced visibly. 'I shouldn't think she would be.'

'No,' agreed Jason hurriedly.

'Why on earth did you do it, son?'

'Because he told me he'd taken Crab.'

'I see. Oh well – I expect they'll be round here soon. Don't you?'

'Yeah. I reckon they will.' Jason then decided to seize an opportunity. 'Dad—'

'Well?'

'Is there something you're keeping back?'

His father looked away from him. 'What do you mean?'

'I mean—'

But the conversation was interrupted annoyingly by a knock at the Segals' front door. Arthur Atkins

55

stood there, his eyes alight with cold anger.

'I hope you're gonna beat him black and blue,' he snarled.

Jason stared at him. Suddenly he felt a twinge of pity for Adam. Now that Arthur Atkins' fury was directed at him personally, he could see how terrifying he was. Thank goodness his dad was there.

'He's been getting an earful from me, and he's sorry. Aren't you, Jason?' His father looked at him intently.

'Sorry, Dad.'

'Sorry, Mr Atkins, it should be,' said Sam firmly.

'Sorry, Mr Atkins,' replied Jason woodenly.

'That ain't enough. My boy's covered in paint, and my wife's having to scour him to get it off.'

Sam nodded. 'Adam wound him up, I think.'

'I don't care what he did. He'd got no call to do that.'

'You're quite right.' Sam spoke quietly. 'I'll give him a thorough telling off. It won't happen again.'

'Adam wants an apology.'

'He won't get one,' said Jason. 'No chance.'

His father sighed and Arthur Atkins snapped, 'If he doesn't apologize, there'll be trouble. I'm not having my boy treated like that.'

'Now wait a minute, Arthur—'

'No. He's been rotten to him ever since we got here.'

'It's mutual,' said Sam quietly.

'We want to make a go of it here, but if your kid doesn't apologize, that's it.'

'I'm sure Eileen wouldn't want to hear you saying that, Arthur,' Sam said, looking worried.

'Wouldn't she?' Arthur was delighted by the reaction he was getting. 'She told me to tell you that she's one hundred per cent behind me.'

'I see.'

Jason felt sorry for his father. He

was sure that Arthur didn't care about Adam's paint-splattered state; he was just enjoying giving Dad a bad time. There was considerable tension between the two men and Jason knew that they would have plenty to say if he wasn't there.

'All right, Dad. I'll apologize to him.' There seemed no other way out.

'Will you, son? That's good of you.'

'It's all I'd expect,' said Arthur smugly. 'Come on then.'

'Go and get it over, son.'

'Yes, Dad.'

Jason slowly followed Arthur and his dad out of the flat and on to the pier. He felt very gloomy for he realized that he had really dropped his dad in it, and that was definitely playing into Arthur Atkins' hands.

Adam was sitting in the Atkins' kitchen, his face red and raw. Eileen had obviously gone back to her client and Arthur was presumably in charge of the cleaning-up operation.

'He's come to say he's sorry,' said Arthur.

'Yeah. I'm sorry about that.' Jason's voice was expressionless.

'So you should be,' sniffed Adam. 'I'll get you for this,' he continued, looking down at the paint which was still thick on his arms.

'Any time.'

'OK then.'

'Look, you two.' It was Arthur's turn to be unwilling referee. 'You've got to stop this now. Right? You listen to me, Adam, or I'll give you one.'

'OK, Dad,' said Adam, very quickly, but his smouldering eyes gazed straight into Jason's. It was open warfare now.

CHAPTER SIX

'Jason.'

'Yes, Dad?'

'Take over the rifle range, will you? Fred's off sick. Usual trouble.' The Segals had inherited Fred with the pier. He'd been there all his life, so he said, but was of little use now.

'The drink?'

'That's it.'

Jason didn't mind. He liked taking over the range – checking the guns, handing out the pellets, setting up the targets and giving out the prizes. Dad was fair: the targets went down and the prizes were good value, unlike other ranges where it was all fixed.

It was seven in the evening now, but a light rain was coming down and business was slack, so he had time to lean up against the side of the shack that housed the range and relax. It formed one side of Madame Zorza's fortune-telling booth and suddenly Jason realized that he could dimly pick up a conversation – and it didn't sound much like fortune-telling. Instantly he was alert, hoping no punters would appear and interrupt him.

'Yeah, it's all set up,' said the thin sound that came through the wall.

'We can do one more job from here – and that's it.'

'This is the biggest.' It was a man's voice, coarse and confident.

'So it may be,' replied Eileen, 'but we've got to be careful. His kid's snooping, and he's a clever little ferret. Sam will see to everything

61

though.' She sounded confident and Jason felt a slow chill of fear. What did she mean? Sam would see to everything?

'You mean he'll shut the kid up?'

'Yes, he won't want to upset Arthur – you know that.'

'It'll be tomorrow night, but there's only one problem.'

'What's that?' Eileen's voice was sharp.

'We can't move the stuff immediately.'

'You'll have to.'

'Not for twenty-four hours.'

'You mean we're going to have the money here for that length of time?'

'It's the only way.' He was surly now.

'Why?'

'We need more time for things to cool off.' He sounded smug, almost wallowing in the difficulties he was creating for her.

'You're sure it's only going to be for twenty-four hours?' She was clearly getting rattled but Jason was even more so. What was his dad mixed up in? What were the Atkins forcing on him?

There was silence and then the man said resentfully, 'I usually deal direct with Arthur. Don't like this fortune-telling bit. You sure your hidey-hole's absolutely OK?' he added sharply.

'Yes, Mr Weston, it's absolutely OK.'

Jason gave a start. Weston. That was the name that had been mentioned when Arthur and Eileen had been battling with the van.

'Oi – you!' A voice rapped out just behind Jason and he spun round unwillingly. A couple of punters were standing by the rifle range, looking angry.

'You running this outfit?' asked the taller of the two men.

'Er – yeah.'

'Well, let's have a couple of rifles then.'

Jason handed them out as if he was a robot and forgot to give the men any pellets.

'Anything to go in 'em?'

'Eh?'

'Ammunition?'

'Sorry.' He handed it over and then leant back against the boarding as the punters began shooting. But all he could hear the other side was a deafening silence.

As soon as he could, Jason hurried back to the flat. He had to find his dad and talk to him. Now. Instead, he found Gran busy preparing tea in the kitchen. When she saw him, she looked up, concerned and worried.

'You all right, love?'

'Yeah.'

'Fancy covering Adam in paint!' She gave him a grim smile. 'You shouldn't have done it.'

Jason fidgeted irritably. Where was his dad? He had to see him. Now.

'I can see why you get angry with that boy.' She sighed. 'He's a rotten

little . . . But I'm sure his dad knocks
him around and—'

'Gran—'

'I'm cooking your favourite supper.
Baked beans and—'

'Where's Dad?' Jason broke in
urgently.

Immediately she looked alarmed.
'What's up?'

'I just want to talk to him that's
all.' For a moment Jason wondered if
he could confide in his gran. It would
be marvellous as she was a really

strong character – the strongest of them all. But he knew he couldn't. Not now. It was his dad he had to see.

'I think he went down the beach,' she said.

'One thing, Gran—' He *had* to say something to her.

'Well?'

'Dad seems almost afraid of Arthur, doesn't he? I've kept noticing that ever since the Atkins arrived.'

'Rubbish.' She scowled at him, but her weathered old face suddenly looked afraid. 'Don't be long,' she snapped. 'Your tea will be ready in half an hour.'

Sam was standing by Crab's pool, staring down at the water, when Jason caught up with him. But more significantly, Jason's mum was with him. What were they doing standing together so miserably? What was going on?

Jason plunged in without any further thought. He knew he had to act fast.

'Dad – Mum—'

They looked up and he was shocked to see the expressions on their faces. They had obviously been talking and both of them looked worried sick.

'The Atkins.'

'What now?' Although she had been looking exhausted recently, Winnie was still usually tough and determined. Now she looked as broken-up as Sam did.

'They really are up to something – Eileen was talking to someone in her fortune-telling booth – they were on about moving stuff and – honest, Dad – Mum – we've *got* to do something. It was Weston who was with them. He's a crook, just like she and Arthur are. They mentioned Weston when—' His voice came to a grinding halt as he stared at his tormented parents.

His father looked at his mother, and she looked away down into the pool again.

Then she turned back to Jason.

'Look, son, we're in a tricky situation and for the moment there's nothing we can do about it. Absolutely nothing. It's not that—' She broke off and half sobbed.

Jason was shocked. He hadn't seen his mum cry in years. 'Tell me, Mum. I've got a *right* to know. And why don't we go to the police?'

'How about coming fishing tomorrow?' his dad asked quietly, putting his arm round Jason's shoulders. 'We can talk then.'

'On the *Morning Glory*?'

'Yes.'

'Great.'

There was a pause, then Jason said, 'How long will Arthur and Eileen stay with us, Dad?'

'We'll talk tomorrow,' he repeated firmly, putting his arm round Winnie. 'Don't worry, old girl,' he said gently. 'We'll see it through.'

'But for how long?' She gave that awful half-sob again and Jason ran off, back to the pier. He just couldn't bear to see her so unhappy.

*

The sea was very calm as the *Morning Glory* slipped from the steeply rising beach on to the glassy surface. There was a very slight mist, but it soon parted as if pushed aside by the prow of the fishing boat.

'We'll put the nets down in about half an hour,' said Dad. 'I'll just slip below and make some tea. You take over the wheel.'

Jason steered the *Glory* out to sea. There wasn't a breath of wind anywhere and there were no other boats to be seen at all. Keeping one eye on the compass and the other on their course, Jason watched the dark green slapping water, wondering when his father was going to talk to him. He hadn't slept well and had spent most of the night wondering how his parents had ever got caught up in the Atkins' web.

'Here we go.' His dad was beside him, big and burly, with two cups of strong tea sweetened by condensed milk. Great stuff – they always had

this on their rare trips in the *Glory*. Gran wouldn't make it at home. 'Filthy muck,' she called it and that was that.

'Hello.' There was a different note in his dad's voice; he sounded apprehensive and uncertain. 'She's still around.'

Jason followed his gaze and saw another fishing boat on the horizon.

Sam grabbed the wheel and set a different course.

'Dad—'

'Mm?'

'What's going on? You said you were going to tell me.' Jason felt he had to take the initiative. He just couldn't bear the suspense any more.

There was a long silence and Jason saw that his dad looked worried and almost trapped as his strong hands grasped the wheel.

'The Atkins. What have they got on you? And what's strange about that fishing boat? It seems perfectly

normal to me.' Jason looked at him expectantly.

There was another long silence.

'Dad!'

'All right then.'

Jason relaxed and so did his father. They both knew the waiting game was over.

'This musn't go any further.'

'No.'

'Only your mum knows what's going on – and your gran has guessed some of it. But they're both strong women, Jason, as you know. They're biding their time.'

'Dad—' Jason was in an agony of suspense. 'Please!'

'OK. Some time ago, before I met your mum, I got into a bit of trouble.'

'Yeah?'

'I nicked some money. I was stony-broke – and, well, I was a fool. I nicked it off a fairground boss. A showman. And they're powerful, I tell you that. They've also got elephant memories. Might have been fifteen years ago, but that would be yesterday to this guy if Arthur told him I'd been involved.'

'But where does Atkins come in?'

'All too often. He was my partner.'

'In the robbery?'

'Yeah. We were both caught by the police. But I gave them the slip, and Arthur couldn't quite make it. He did time.'

'But didn't he grass you up?'

'No, he didn't. He did a stretch and came out. I thought I'd seen the last of him – put it all behind me. But he came down here. He saved it all up for me, do you see? It's like taking revenge plus having a nice safe haven. And he's up to something else now, but I swear to you, Jason, I'm not involved. I don't know what he's doing, who this man Weston is, or what they're trying to hide here. I just haven't a clue.'

'I believe you, Dad.'

'You'd better! All I can hope is that the Atkins *do* go to sunny Spain soon. Don't tell me to go to the police. I just daren't. I don't want to serve time for what I did all those years ago, and Arthur would grass me up now with the greatest of pleasure if I didn't help him out.'

Jason nodded. He was quite sure he would. But how would his father *ever* get out of his clutches? 'I'm really glad you've told me all this. I knew there was something wrong.'

'You're a clever little so-and-so, aren't you?'

'What about the fishing boat then?'

'Yeah, well, that's suspicious. She's been around for a few days and none of the locals have seen her before. What's more, she never puts down her nets.'

'Blimey. Do you think she's something to do with this bloke Weston?'

'I told you, I haven't the faintest idea. Maybe she's waiting for something – like she's on standby.'

'You think—' began Jason.

'I reckon Arthur's loot might be going on it. Eventually.'

'And Arthur, would he be going on it too?' asked Jason tentatively.

'I wish he would. The sooner he clears off the better.'

'So what do we do, Dad?' asked Jason. He felt a great sense of relief now he knew something at least of what was going on.

'Nothing.'

'What do you mean?'

'Like your mum and gran, I want to bide my time. Because if the police catch him in the act then he's still going to grass me up, isn't he? It'll be a straight race between the police and that fairground boss – and if I had my choice I'd rather have the police win. See what I mean, Jason?'

Jason did see what his father meant, all too well. He felt an awful sinking in the pit of his stomach for he knew how much, either way, his father was going to suffer. But he was still determined to nail the Atkins.

'Dad?' Jason asked cautiously.

'Yes?'

'Can I keep watch on the Atkins? Find out what they're really up to?'

'You leave that to me, son. I'll be doing all that.'

'How can you? You said you were biding your time.'

'I've got my ways. Now listen, Jason—' His father looked extremely worried. 'I *had* to tell you what I've just told you, but don't think I liked doing it. You've got to keep out of the

Atkins' way and not go spying on them or do anything else. Do you get me?'

'I get you, Dad,' said Jason doubtfully.

'So what are you going to do?'

'Keep out of the Atkins' way, Dad.'

'You'd better,' said his father, ferociously. 'We've got to wait – just do nothing.'

But Jason had no intention of doing nothing.

CHAPTER SEVEN

When they had winched the *Morning Glory* up the beach just after lunch, Sam Segal again warned Jason not to get involved and once again he assured his father that he wouldn't.

Later, he wandered down to the beach and knelt by Crab's pool.

'Crab,' he called gently.

There was no movement.

'Crab.' He had been caught this way before, imagining all kinds of awful things had happened to Crab.

'Crab.'

Still nothing.

'Crab!' He stared down into the water. It was quite clear and there was absolutely no sign of him at all. Where was he? 'Crab?' He shifted rocks, debris, seaweed, urchins, anemones, but the crab wasn't there. Suddenly, all the pressure of the day – his father's confession and indecisions, his own determination to unmask the Atkins – came together in a burning rage. 'Adam!' he bellowed. 'This time I'll kill you!'

Jason ran towards the pier, yelling Adam's name. He'd done it this time, he told himself over and over again. Adam had really gone and done it now. Crab – his one magical talisman in the face of grim adversity – had gone.

He pounded up the ramp, pushed his way through the customers around the dressed-crab stand and confronted Adam who was helping his mother.

'I'll give you five seconds.'

'Eh?'

'Five.'

'Don't know what you're on about.'

As had happened before, a curious little crowd began to gather.

'Yes, you do. Where is he?'

'Who?'

'Crab.'

'Your little mate? Oh – I dressed him.' He giggled unpleasantly. 'I boiled him first though. Look, he's gone a nice red colour.'

Jason's fist shot out and connected

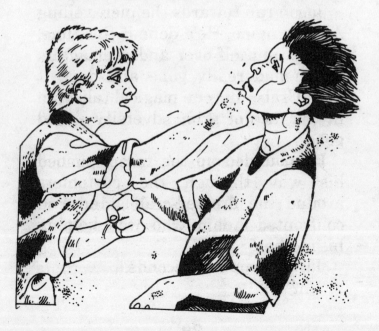

forcibly with Adam's chin, and he went down on the ground, howling with rage.

'Not again,' said Eileen, her dark eyes flashing with venom. 'Sam!' she screamed. 'Get over here.'

Sam Segal arrived from the rifle range at the double as the crowd, scenting blood, increased.

'He went for him again,' said Eileen.

'Jason, what's happened now?' Sam asked wearily.

'He's broken my nose,' wailed Adam, as the blood flowed down his chin.

'Paint one day, blood the next,' roared Eileen. 'What's he want to do? Kill my boy?'

'Now listen you—' Sam furiously addressed his son.

'He's got Crab,' panted Jason.

'Don't start that again,' she said.

'I never touched him,' moaned Adam, trying to wipe the blood off his nose and failing.

'You've got him,' returned Jason truculently. 'You've got him and I want him.'

'Just a minute.'

They all wheeled round to see Gran walking down the pier in an apron with her sleeves rolled up.

'What's going on?' she yelled. 'I heard all this noise and – are you all right, Jason?'

'Go away, you stupid old woman!' Eileen was beside herself with rage. Somehow Gran's aggression and protection of Jason finally made her lose control completely. 'Jason!' she shouted. 'He's attacked my son.'

The crowd pressed closer, sensing more trouble, and Adam, deprived of attention, began to cry loudly.

'No need for you to interfere, Madame Zorza, you big fake,' snapped Gran, also losing her temper. Jason knew that she had had a very long fuse over the Atkins but now it had burnt itself out.

'I beg your pardon?' said Eileen,

trying to appear in control of the situation.

'You've never told a fortune in your life.'

'I'll have you know—'

'Don't you remember those days at Fiddlers' Fair in Edmonton?'

'I'll have you know—' repeated Eileen.

'You're a fake, Eileen Atkins, and that's all there is to it.' There was a delighted intake of breath from the eager crowd as she turned to her son. 'Goodness knows why you ever employed *her* in the first place,' she snapped, but Sam didn't reply. He simply closed his eyes, knowing worse was to follow.

'I am Madame Zorza,' said Eileen indignantly.

'And as you know, I was Vera the Visionary,' rapped back Jason's grandmother. 'I was a *genuine* fortune-teller, and my mother before me, and her mother before that. Let me tell you, I know a fake when I see one.' She turned to Sam. 'Don't I, son?'

Sam looked as if he wished the boards of the pier would suddenly snap and throw him thankfully into the sea.

'*Don't* I?'

'You've been in the business a long time, Mum. But I really don't think you should—'

'Are you going to—' But Gran broke off as Jason suddenly yelled at Adam again.

'Where *is* he – where's Crab?'

'You'll never know.' He sniffed, dabbing his bloodied nose. 'Never.'

'He'll be in your room, won't he?' Jason was guessing wildly.

'Yeah?'

'I'll go and look.'

'You won't! Mum, he's going to break into our flat.'

But Jason was already off, leaving Eileen and Sam to yell after him.

As Jason disappeared into the rooms behind the bingo parlour,

Gran turned back to her son. 'I want an answer from you, Sam Segal,' she said furiously. 'Do I know a fake when I see one, or don't I?' Her gimlet eye bored into him as he began to flounder, and Eileen smiled a secret smile at Sam's embarrassment. The crowd listened with bated breath.

The front door of the Atkins' flat was open and Jason darted in, heading straight for what he guessed was Adam's untidy and rather smelly bedroom. For a moment he could only make out a jumble of old clothes and broken toys. Then, with a whoop of relief, Jason saw Crab in a glass tank on Adam's windowsill, his heart-shaped mark clearly identifying him. He was crouched at the bottom and looking doleful, but at least he didn't seem to have come to any harm.

'Crab. You OK?'

Crab looked up at him, eyes staring, a claw slightly moving.

'I'll get you out.'

He picked up the tank – it wasn't very big – and hurried outside again. The crowd was draining fitfully away but Gran was still there, arguing with Dad and Eileen Atkins. Adam was snivelling, quite left out of the action.

'What's this then?' asked Jason as he arrived with the tank and Crab, now passive on the gravelled bottom.

'Well? What now?' Gran was bewildered. 'What's that crab doing? What's that got to do with anything?'

'What indeed?' asked Sam with rising anger. 'Adam, did you put this crab in the tank?'

'Well?' asked Eileen, obviously feeling attacked on all sides. 'What you been up to, Adam?'

'You pinched him from the pool and put him in the tank on your bedroom windowsill, didn't you? Just to spite me.' Jason's voice was hard and triumphant.

Adam hung his head and his nose started bleeding again.

'Speak up, boy,' said Eileen. 'Did you or didn't you?'

'It was very cruel if he did,' pronounced Sam. 'Did you?'

Slowly, Adam nodded.

'Do I know a fake when I see one or not?' asked Gran, piling on the agony. 'I've had enough of you, Eileen Atkins—'

'I've never been so insulted—'

Jason had an overpowering urge to laugh uncontrollably as he marched proudly past them all, Crab's tank in his hands. He had fought a battle and won. Now he had to fight a bigger one, but saving Crab was important. Crab was his talisman, and it was Crab who was going to help him beat the Atkins.

He knelt down by the pool, seeing that the water was scummy and muddy. Obviously Adam had stirred up the pool completely when he kidnapped Crab. Never mind, thought Jason. It'll soon be clear again. He put Crab gently back in the water, rubbing the heart-shaped mark on his shell as he did so. Somehow he thought that might bring him good luck. He needed some badly enough.

CHAPTER EIGHT

Jason sat dejectedly by Crab's pool. He looked at his watch; it was just coming up to half-past four and it wouldn't be dark for ages. If only something would happen. But everything looked depressingly normal except that Adam was no longer behind the dressed-crab stall. Jason could just make out a notice that said *TEMPORARILY CLOSED – REOPENING IN AN HOUR.* No doubt Adam was still receiving first-aid to his nose or was recovering somewhere. Adam had really got it in the neck from his parents – and from Sam – and the punch Jason had given him seemed to have been temporarily overlooked. He stared up towards the bingo parlour and someone ducked down. It had to be Adam. He was probably plotting again as hard as he could, but what did Jason care? Adam was just an irritating speck in the whirlpool of his thoughts. Then he saw a familiar figure walking slowly along the beach, bent, withered but purposeful.

'Where've you been, Gran?' he asked as she came up to him.

'Having a think,' she grumbled. 'Like you, I guess.'

Jason didn't know what to say. How much did she know? he wondered. He daren't reveal what his dad had told him on the *Morning Glory*, but he was desperate to talk to someone – and Gran had often been his real friend when there was trouble at home. She had lived with them so long now that she was just as important to him as his parents.

'I hate those Atkins,' he said. 'I know they're crooks.'

She nodded but didn't say anything.

'I want to get them!'

'Be careful.' She sat down beside him with painful slowness. 'Old bones,' she muttered. 'How's your crab?'

'He's all right now, but I'm scared that prat, Adam, is going to get him. He hates me. You know that.'

'I don't know where all this is going to end,' she said. 'I really don't know.'

'I'm scared of something else, Gran,' admitted Jason.

'What's that, son?' She put her arm round his shoulder and he cuddled up to her, needing her comfort and wisdom.

'Those Atkins – they've got it in for Dad, haven't they?'

'I don't know, Jason.'

'You *do*.'

'Maybe I do.'

'I'd like to sort them out.'

'So would I, Jason. But what can an old woman and a child do?' She sounded as if she was thinking aloud.

'We can do a lot, Gran,' insisted Jason. But he still couldn't think exactly what.

'Wait a minute,' said Gran, clambering stiffly to her feet and staring into the pool. 'Now what's that?'

'Eh?' Jason got up slowly, unwilling to change the subject.

'Blimey,' said Gran. 'This pool's full of money.'

Sure enough, the bottom of the pool was littered with bundles of five pound notes, tied together with elastic bands. Some had broken free and Jason noticed that one of the notes was wrapped around one of Crab's pincers. Jason stared down at Crab disbelievingly. Where could they have come from? Then he remembered how cloudy the pool had been when he put Crab back in. Perhaps that was why he hadn't noticed

anything. Gently stroking Crab on his shell and putting him on a rock, he took the note away from him.

'Well,' said Gran. 'We'd better get 'em out.'

Slowly they began to gather in their sodden haul. They were in the middle of this when a gratingly familiar voice broke into their harvesting.

'What have you got there then? Crab's Midland Bank?' Arthur Atkins stood there smiling. But there was not the slightest ounce of humour in the smile – only a dark anger of considerable venom.

CHAPTER NINE

'Give me those.' He crouched down and began to gather up the notes. 'That Adam's for the high jump.' His eyes narrowed unpleasantly, and Jason felt an unusual rush of sympathy for Adam. It must be awful having Atkins for a father.

'Why?' asked Gran. 'What's he done?'

'This is mine – the day's take on the bookmaking. That wretched boy of mine's dumped it in the pool.'

'What a strange thing to do,' remarked Gran, looking very suspicious.

'Not really. He wants to pay us out, doesn't he. Just because I gave him a damn good hiding.'

Arthur continued to gather up his wringing-wet fivers, plunging his hand into the pool and talking fast.

'He got up this morning and we had a row about how much I was paying him to run the dressed-crab stall. Didn't think it was enough, the little so-and-so. So what did he do? He nicked the take – like I say, just to spite me. Shoved it in this pool. I'll learn him.'

'Don't go too hard on him,' said Gran. 'He's only a kid.'

Arthur sneered up at her. 'I'll thank you to mind your own business, Mrs Segal. You've caused enough trouble.'

'By the way,' said Gran casually. 'I saw you got a major delivery this morning. Very early this morning. About five, wasn't it?'

Jason stared at her. She obviously

didn't realize what she was saying.

'Eh?' Arthur gazed at her very uneasily and then began to scrabble in the water again.

'All those boxes that came out of that battered old van. What was in them?'

'If you *must* know, they were bingo cards. That's the last one,' he wheezed as he hauled out the final sodden roll of fivers. 'Thanks for being so observant.' He laughed briefly; it was a particularly unpleasant sound. Then Arthur turned on his heel and walked away, clutching the money to his chest.

'Well,' said Gran. 'That stinks.'

'You mean it's not the take?'

'You ought to come clean with me, Jason,' said Gran crossly. 'You know more than you're letting on.'

'I don't.'

'You do, my lad. You'd better tell me – it'll be safe with me.'

'Well—'

'Come on!' she said sternly.

'Dad said I mustn't.'

'Did he now? Well, he's my son so I completely overrule him. Now what's the story?'

Jason began to pour it all out to Gran, about the prison sentence and the showman and Arthur's revenge, and then he began to repeat it all over again. Eventually Gran held up a hand and stopped him.

'Thank you, Jason.'

'Don't tell Dad I told you.'

'I won't,' she said quietly.

'Did you know any of that?' asked Jason anxiously.

'A bit. I knew your dad had been in trouble but I didn't know why, and I didn't know he'd got mixed up with Arthur. I suppose your mum knows the full story?'

'Yes.'

'Well – she's a good woman. She'll see him through – or try to.' She sighed. 'I can see why they tried to keep it from me – to save me worrying and all that. But I'm not such an old fool as they think. I guessed something was up. Now I understand why Arthur looked so upset when I said I'd seen the van arrive this morning.' Then she paused and a gleam came into her eye. 'Well, Jason. How about us being partners?'

'What in, Gran?'

'In fixing those Atkins – what else? We're going to bring them to justice, you and I.'

Jason stared at her disbelievingly, but she looked so ferociously confident that a sudden hope sprung up inside him. 'Can we?' he asked wonderingly.

'Yes,' said Gran. 'We certainly can – and we'll start straight away. Suppose those boxes are full of fivers – thousands of 'em. Even Arthur Atkins can't explain away that much as a bookie's take.'

'Where are those boxes?' asked Jason slowly.

'Guess where? They all went into Eileen's fortune-telling booth. Now, if I cause a bit of a fuss, how about you slipping in there and having a butchers?'

'Blimey,' said Jason.

'Well, we partners or not?' asked Gran.

'We're partners all right,' said Jason, and he shook Gran's hand.

'OK.' Gran began to march towards the pier and Jason followed in her wake. 'We'll have to wait until she's alone – without a client – and then strike.' Rather breathlessly, she began to tell Jason what they had to do.

Half an hour later, Gran lowered her binoculars. From the kitchen window of the Segals' flat, she could see down the length of the pier and spot any comings and goings outside Madame Zorza's booth.

'That's one punter out and there's no-one else waiting. This is our chance. Leg it.'

When Gran moved fast she really moved, and Jason had a job keeping up with her as she marched down the wooden boarding like an avenging warrior.

'I'll cause the trouble right away,' she muttered. 'And you do what we planned.'

'Suppose she goes for you, Gran?'

'Then I'll go for her. Nothing would give me greater satisfaction.'

Jason grinned. He knew she meant what she said.

'Eileen!' Gran yelled outside Madame Zorza's booth. 'Come out of there, sharpish.'

'Who's that?' came a muffled voice.

'Who else but Vera the Visionary.'

'What do *you* want?'

'I'm going to tell everyone on this pier that you're nothing but a blooming great fake.'

'I beg your pardon?'

'You heard.'

'Go away.'

'Not till I get some satisfaction,' yelled Gran. 'And that means exposing you for what you are.'

Jason noticed that a small crowd was gathering and he felt a chill of fear. Gran was going to be in big trouble for this. And what would the Atkins do to Dad?

'Get lost.' Eileen poked her head out of the booth. She was puffing on a fag and had a very nasty look in her eye. 'You've been told not to bother me like this. Go away or it'll be the worse for your precious son.'

'Come out,' Gran challenged. 'Come out and face the public. Fake!' She turned to the eagerly gathering crowd. 'This woman's a fake!' she yelled. 'She can no more tell your fortune than she can run a hundred metres. She's not even a paid-up member of the Fortune-Tellers' Association.'

'There's no such thing,' Eileen said coldly as she ground out her cigarette with her stiletto heel. 'Now – on your bike, you old ratbag.'

'Take your crystal ball,' shouted Gran, 'and shove it up your right nostril. It should be a good fit.'

'How dare you talk to me like that, you – you awful old wizened hag.'

Someone in the crowd cheered, but Jason shivered. Where was all this going to end?

It wasn't long before Eileen Atkins finally emerged from her booth. Gran went up to her and stood in her path.

'Get out of my way,' Eileen shouted.

'Make me. Fake.'

'You really are a very stupid old crone, aren't you?' Eileen Atkins' eyes flashed hatred.

'Fake.'

'I'm going to see your son. To complain.'

'Fake,' Gran goaded.

She shoved Gran hard in the chest and pushed past her. 'I'm going to get

Sam to have you certified,' she snarled. 'You're nothing but a public nuisance.'

Eileen hurried up to the Segals' flat and hammered on the door, followed by the crowd. Meanwhile Gran winked at Jason and he slipped quickly into the booth.

CHAPTER TEN

Jason knew he only had a few minutes, maybe less, and as he desperately glanced round the cluttered and rather grubby interior of Eileen's booth, his gaze took in crystal balls, star charts, dirty teacups, torn cloaks covered with the signs of the zodiac, and piles of old newspapers. There were a couple of canvas chairs, a scarred card table and a teapot. Towards the back there was a huge wooden cupboard, the usual contents of which, largely books on *How to be a Palmist, an Astrologer, a*

Fortune-Teller, were strewn about on the floor.

Jason turned to the cupboard and, sure enough, jammed inside were dozens of cardboard boxes. He began to pull them out, knowing instantly that they were strangely, disappointingly, light.

He ripped off the lids to find that the first, the second, the third and the fourth were empty. Quickly replacing them, he pulled out more and more and more. But they were all empty. Almost sobbing with disappointment, Jason threw them back in the cupboard and was just about to wrench out some more when he heard not only Eileen's strident voice, but his dad's as well, raised in apology.

'I'm *not* putting up with it,' she was raving. 'The boy's bad enough, but that old woman's even worse. She's like an interfering little kid herself – and just as abusive. Your mother's had the audacity to doubt my credentials and I can tell you I shall require a written apology.'

'Yes – yes,' Dad was saying smoothly. 'This is all most unfortunate.'

'It will be, for you,' she replied in a sinister voice, and Jason heard his father pause.

'Look, Eileen – I'm sure this can all be sorted out—'

Jason didn't wait to hear any more, for he knew if he was caught in there it wouldn't just be him for the high jump. He plunged towards the door.

Tea-time in the Segal household was a very tense affair, for neither he nor his gran were exactly in favour.

'You *must* stop this feuding, Jason,' his mum snapped. Her face was working and there were tears in her eyes. She had obviously been thinking over recent events and was still thoroughly upset.

'Feuding?' he repeated defensively.

'You know what she means,' said Dad irritably.

'You've got to stop,' said Mum, getting up and disconsolately making her way out to the kitchen where she clattered and crashed the dishes. But they could also hear that she was crying.

'Now look what you've done,' said Dad, and then he lowered his voice. 'She doesn't know I told you, so leave it out.'

'You *know* what they're doing.'

'I said, leave it out.'

Jason wondered whether or not he should tell his dad that he had confesed everything to Gran, but before he could say anything, his father also rose to his feet. 'I've had it up to here,' he muttered. 'So leave the Atkins alone. And that's an order.'

But Jason could see the desperation in his eyes. Leave them alone? Why – he was only just beginning.

*

Jason watched television for a while but all he saw in the flickering images were the distorted features of Arthur, Eileen and Adam Atkins. After a while he was so tired that he went to bed where he quickly dropped off to sleep and dreamed about searching for the loot that the Atkins had hidden.

He saw himself running off the pier and over the beach, down to Crab's pool. When he gazed into it, he saw that the water was suddenly very deep and that there was a huge chest at the bottom that Crab was sitting on. He waved his pincers at Jason and, as he did so, Jason felt himself pitched into the cold, clear water by a hard shove in the back. He twisted and turned as he sank below the surface, and as he looked up he saw Arthur Atkins' face, dark and shimmering, his mouth open in a great shout of laughter.

With his lungs bursting, Jason hit

the chest and the lid burst open. Five pound notes showered up at him, wrapping themselves round him in freezing coils until he was covered in them from head to foot. He fought and struggled until the heaviness of the paper money wrapped him in a cocoon, dragging him down, down into the chest. It was then that Jason woke up and found himself struggling in his sheets.

Gradually, calming down and wiping the sweat from his eyes, he tried to sleep again but it was impossible. Jason then lay awake for what seemed like hours until he thought he heard a shout. He clambered stiffly out of bed and turned to the window. There was a full moon and silver light streamed down on the pier and the ragged rows of tall fishermen's drying sheds beyond. Then he saw two figures, one small and struggling, the other like a fox in the night carrying away its prey. There was not the slightest doubt in Jason's

mind as to whom they were – Adam
and Arthur. What on earth could be
going on?

CHAPTER ELEVEN

Jason watched Adam stop struggling as Arthur cuffed him round the head. He staggered and then they both stopped outside one of the sheds. Arthur fumbled for a key, inserted it, wrenched open the door – and flung Adam inside. Then he closed and locked the shed again. The whole operation was over in seconds and Arthur walked quietly away, a satisfied look on his narrow face. There was complete silence behind him and Jason was surprised that there was no hammering on the door.

What was Adam doing in there? Why wasn't he trying to escape?

Jason wondered what he was going to do next. Should he go and try to rescue Adam? Of course he had to, but what would his own parents say? Wasn't he plunging himself even further into the dubious affairs of the Atkins? Well, of course he was. But however much he disliked Adam, Jason knew he couldn't possibly leave him there, so he left his bedroom very quietly, ran lightly down the stairs and cautiously unlocked the door.

There was a damp, chilling breeze blowing outside and Jason paused, almost deciding to go back in again. But how could he? Decisively, he hurried down the length of the pier, keeping a wary eye out for Arthur, but there was no sign or sound of anyone. The beach had a bleached-out look in the moonlight and looked horribly exposed, but Jason made the tall shed in seconds. Then he hesitated. What should he do? Knock? Call? And was Arthur lurking nearby?

'Adam!'

There was no reply.

'Adam.' Jason hissed the word as near to the door as he could manage. Then he heard a sob.

'Adam!'

'Who is it?'

'Jason. What are you doing in there?'

'Dad locked me in.'

'Why?'

'I woke up and saw him going out. I followed him, but he must have heard me. Anyway, he turned round and grabbed me and locked me in here. He'll be back in the morning.' Adam gave another strangled sob. 'I'll be OK. Honest.'

'I'm coming in,' said Jason determinedly.

'He's taken the key.'

'Wait.'

'I'm not going anywhere.'

Jason ran round the back of the shed. It was in poor condition, and a good number of its boards were rotten, so it was not a difficult job to begin to prise up some of the wood. Eventually, Jason made a big enough hole to squeeze through.

The darkness was almost impenetrable as Jason stumbled around in the fishy-smelling space. Then he tripped, sprawling over a soft, warm object.

'Ouch!' said Adam.

'Come on. Let's get out.'

'Dad'll kill me. I'd rather stay here. I told you not to come in.' He sounded aggrieved.

Meanwhile, Jason's eyes were gradually becoming used to the blackness and he was beginning to make out that there were large boxes stacked round the walls.

'What's in those?' he asked.

'Nothing.'

'They look new.'

Adam rose to his feet. 'Go on,' he said in a feeble attempt to threaten Jason. 'Clear off and mind your own business.' But he was clearly in no state to be aggressive and he staggered slightly as he stood there.

'What's in them?' repeated Jason.

'I don't know. Nothing.'

'I'm going to have a look.'

'No.' But Adam made no move towards him as Jason grabbed the end of one of the boxes and pulled hard. At first the cardboard resisted, but when he pulled even harder something made of crisp and crackling paper emerged from one end.

'Blimey,' said Jason.

He had in his hand a five pound note.

'They're full of 'em,' said Adam mournfully. 'He'll kill me though if he finds out you've been here and looked in those boxes.'

'No, he won't,' replied Jason with sudden decision. 'I'm going to get him nicked.'

'Then what will happen to me?' wailed Adam.

'Your mum will look after you, won't she?'

'She'll get nicked too. She's in it with him.' Adam sniffed. 'I'll be as good as an orphan. I'll have nowhere to go.'

He began to cry again very noisily. Jason felt slightly embarrassed but he knew he had to shut Adam up fast before he was heard. But how?

Suddenly he had an idea. 'You'll

have to come and live with us then.'

'What?' Adam was astounded, and dubious.

'Come and live with us,' Jason repeated firmly. What was he saying? Was he crazy? 'Mum and Dad and Gran won't mind. They'll always help people in trouble.'

'My parents could be inside for years. And we don't get on.'

'We can try.' Jason thought hard. Could they? Or would they fight all the time? But there was no time for consideration for he knew that if he didn't reassure Adam now, he would have no chance of bringing Arthur and Eileen to justice. Then another thought struck him. Arthur would still take a terrible revenge on Dad. Would he be sent to prison too, after being grassed up? Indecision filled Jason. What was he going to do? Desperately he gazed at Adam. Then he said, 'I know.'

'What?' Adam looked at him very suspiciously.

'Maybe there's a way out,' he said vaguely, knowing there wasn't. 'Your dad's got some kind of hold on mine.'

Adam nodded.

'Suppose he promises to go away, leave us in peace, take the money with him—' His voice weakened. 'I won't shop him if he leaves my dad alone.'

'That won't work,' said Adam confidently.

'No?'

'No chance. My dad's too cunning. I know the hold he's got – and he'll keep it. He'll make sure of that.'

'But if – if I go to the police,' Jason's voice shook, 'he'll tell on him and my dad will be in prison too.'

Adam thought for a while and then said softly, 'I reckon if it's *your* dad who hands him over with all this money, they'll go pretty easy on him. Don't you?'

'Maybe.'

'And that's the best deal you'll get.' Adam was firm.

'You sure?'

'Yeah, and what's more—' He hesitated. 'Do you really mean it?'

'About you coming to live with us? I promise I do.' Jason knew he was stuck with the offer now. They would just have to make the best of what might be a really bad job.

'But what about your parents?' asked Adam doubtfully. 'Would they *really* agree?'

'I told you,' said Jason impatiently, 'they'll help anyone who's in trouble.'

'I'd do anything to get away from him,' muttered Adam. 'Mum's not so bad but he really knocks me about. Sometimes I think he might—' He paused, and then carried on, speaking very quietly. 'We'll have to move fast. They'll be here just before dawn.'

'They?'

'The fence. The guy who's going to launder the money. He's coming in by sea.'

'You mean Weston – and the

fishing boat?'

'So she's been noticed,' said Adam almost gleefully. 'And he's a real—Well, we'd better watch out for Weston, that's all. He's meaner than my dad – and that's really saying something.'

Jason nodded. It was difficult to believe, but if Adam said so then he must be right.

'The boat's been noticed hanging around. But what do you mean about them "laundering" the money?'

Adam laughed. 'It means they pay Dad his share by stashing it abroad somewhere in a bank. Then the bank pays out later.'

Jason shrugged. 'I don't get it.'

'It doesn't really matter.' Adam was impatient now. 'Look – we've got to get going. I'll take one of those smaller boxes and show your dad. Then he can ring the police and if they come quick they'll catch them red-handed.'

'OK.' Whatever his doubts, Jason

knew they to act now. And fast.

Once they had both crawled through the gap Jason had made in the wooden planking, they discovered the wind was rising and the white-capped waves were beginning to lash the shore.

'Let's get to the pier,' said Jason, shivering violently.

But Adam's eyes were scanning the beach further away.

'There's a boat coming in.'

'Where?'

'Right up there – far end of the beach – beyond the pier. You can just see it through the girders.' They ducked down behind a bank of pebbles and Jason saw the fishing boat heaving in the swell a few metres out. It looked like a ghost ship – no lights, no engine, no sign of anyone aboard.

'Come *on*, they'll be down here any second,' yelled Jason, his voice almost lost in the roaring of the wind.

But neither of them moved as they

saw someone suddenly leap out of the fishing boat.

'That'll be Weston,' Adam whispered. 'He's got a torch.'

The shadowy figure was heading briskly towards the pier. Then they saw Arthur hurrying down to meet him. The men stood talking by one of the seaweed-festooned girders.

'OK,' said Jason. 'See that boat. It's only a few metres away from them. If we crawl down behind it, we can hear what they're saying.'

'We ought to get to your dad,' moaned Adam.

'How can we? They'll see us. We can do that when they've gone.'

'We'll make too much noise on the pebbles.'

'Come *on*!' Jason grabbed his arm and pulled Adam after him.

Walking on tiptoe they headed for the boat, and Jason was surprised by the very small amount of noise they made. But when they reached some cover and Jason was once again eavesdropping on the men's conversation, he realized why Weston and Arthur Atkins would have been very unlikely to have heard them anyway, for they were in the middle of a blazing row. Their frustration was obviously even greater because they were forced to conduct their argument very quietly but, in spite of the wind, Jason could just hear what they were saying.

'You never said you wanted more,' said Arthur through gritted teeth.

'You don't think I pulled that job on my own, do you? It took money and time and a couple of other blokes.'

'Too bad. You never told me that.'

'And there's the boat. That cost more than I bargained for.'

'You never told me that either. I'm hundreds down.'

'I'm taking what I have to take.' Weston's voice was hard and there was a grim finality to it.

'No you're not.'

There was a long silence while

Jason tried to imagine what was happening.

'So what are you going to do about it?' asked Weston eventually.

'I'll simply take my share. It's all in the drying shed and I've got the key.'

'We'll see about that.'

'You want to settle it now?' asked Arthur.

'Why not?'

There was another long silence during which Jason could feel Adam trembling beside him.

'It'll be all right,' he whispered involuntarily, but his attempt at reassurance was a fatal mistake.

'What's that?' It was Arthur's voice, cutting like a knife through the wind.

'We're going to have to run,' said Adam with surprising calm. 'I know a place where we can hide this box of money — if I can get to it.'

'Come out,' said Weston gently. 'Come out now.'

For a moment they stayed where

they were, then they broke cover, Adam taking the lead as they began to run.

'Get back to the pier and see that Eileen is ready,' said Weston. 'I'll head them off. Isn't that your kid?'

'Yeah,' replied Arthur. 'But I'm not going back to any pier. I'm going to the drying shed.'

'You'd better not take anything out,' yelled Weston, 'or it'll be all the worse for your little boy.'

Arthur shrugged grimly.

Running like the wind, Jason and Adam were just about to pass Crab's pool when Jason tripped and fell, dropping the box which burst open. The bank notes rose up in a cloud like paper birds in the wind; they fluttered everywhere, some flying into the pool.

Jason stared helplessly up at the pier. The lights were on in his parents' flat. Help was near, but far enough away to be useless, for as he looked into Adam's terrified eyes he

127

knew that time had run out for them. He scrambled to his feet and darted here and there, trying to collect five pound notes while Adam cowered motionless on the pebbles behind him. Then it was all over as Weston paused, gasping, beside them. Tall and powerfully built, he was young with beaky features and hard, cold eyes, his long dark hair blowing in the wind.

'What the hell do you think you're doing?' he demanded, staring down at the whirling paper money. He began to gather it up very quickly until he came to the pool.

Jason, meanwhile, had grabbed the box which was still half-full and held it close to his chest.

Weston glared at him angrily and began to move purposefully towards him, but Jason didn't move, his eyes riveted to a rock beside the pool. Following his gaze, Weston caught sight of Crab sitting astride a pile of soggy five pound notes.

Weston grinned. 'I've heard about you,' he said to Jason. 'Aren't you the daft little so-and-so who's got a thing about a crab? And this is the crab, isn't it?'

Jason said nothing as Weston advanced on Crab.

'If you don't give me that box, sonny, I'll crush his shell – and that'll be the end of your little pet,' he said, smiling maliciously.

Jason watched him in horror. Weston could easily have got the box off him. Was he just enjoying being cruel?

'*Please* don't!'

In a quick, vulture-like movement Weston picked up Crab from his rock, together with the bundle of soggy notes.

'Then give me the box. Now!'

With a half-sob, Jason shoved the box at him and Weston flung Crab back into his pool. But just before the man let him go, Crab gave him a vicious nip on the fingers and he let out a howl of pain, dropping the box on the shingle.

Still grunting with pain, Weston's eyes darted around the darkened beach for the money. Then he saw that Adam had grabbed it.

'Come on, son. Give it to me. *Immediately.*' There was real menace in his voice now.

131

'You'll be nicked. You deserve to be nicked.' Somehow Adam had gained a new last-ditch courage. 'I'll give the police this lot – and tell 'em where the rest is.'

'Give it here. Now!' Weston repeated, making a grab at the boy, but already Adam was running up the beach and away from the pier, running as fast as he could, easily outdistancing his pursuer. Jason quickly checked in the pool to make sure Crab hadn't been hurt, and was then about to set off after them when he heard a police siren on the still-mounting wind.

Running down the ramp towards a police car that was pulling up with a squealing of brakes were an oddly assorted group of people. His parents were first, waving torches, followed by a loudly complaining Eileen Atkins. Just behind her was Gran, looking determined.

A second police car drew up at the pier and there was an animated discussion, but Jason had decided not to wait. Adam would be in real trouble if Weston caught up with him. There was something about him that made Jason aware that he would be as ruthless and uncaring as Arthur.

'Help me,' he whispered to Crab, and started off up the beach.

'There he is!' he heard his father shouting, and one of the policemen set off after him. As Jason ran, he looked back over his shoulder and saw Arthur tearing across the beach from the drying sheds. He was heading away from the pier, pursued by another policeman.

The rain began gently and soon became fierce. Heavy clouds covered the face of the moon and the darkness closed in. Jason stumbled as he ran on, head down in the face of the still rising, buffeting wind. Eventually the rain became so heavy that it was like running through the sea, and the thunder of the waves became louder as the wind intensified. He could hardly see ahead of him, and the white horses out at sea seemed to become glowing illuminations. Almost phosphorescent in their dazzling whiteness, they seemed to light the beach with an eerie glow.

Then he saw the old battered sign, WAVECREST CAFE, and underneath it, in even more faded letters, LIGHT LUNCHEONS, CRAB TEAS. Could this be the hiding place Adam had been heading for in his desperate bid to outrun Weston and hide the box? Through the pouring rain, Jason could dimly make out the weathered old clapboard building, long deserted, battered by the elements, with a hole in the roof and the windows boarded up.

Jason slowed down to a walk, but as he approached, he couldn't see a sign of either of them. They seemed to have completely disappeared, swallowed up in the swirling, clamorous night.

CHAPTER TWELVE

Around the derelict Wavecrest Cafe
was a mound of stones and pebbles,
washed up into high banks. Jason
paused and listened. He couldn't hear
a sound apart from the wind. Where
on earth were they? They couldn't
have just disappeared. He wasn't
that far behind them. If they were
still running he should be able to
hear their feet scrunching on the
pebbles.

'Psst.' The low sound seemed to
float out from behind the shingle to
the left of the building.

'Who's that?'

'It's Adam.'

'Where are you?' hissed Jason.

'Behind the bank.'

Jason found Adam crouched in a hollow. He was shivering.

'Weston – he's looking for me round the back. I haven't had time to hide the money.'

'Where's the box?' rapped Jason.

'I'm sitting on it.'

'The police are coming,' said Jason, kneeling down beside him. 'We'll be all right.'

But even as he spoke, there was an angry roar and Weston suddenly appeared on top of the bank of pebbles, his long lean body poised to spring and his craggy face, almost covered by his long dark hair, twisted in vicious fury.

With a wailing cry Adam got up, dodged and ran as hard as he could over the pebbles towards the boiling sea, the cardboard box still firmly clutched in his hands. Weston followed in long-legged pursuit. Adam had waded out quite a way but Weston was already beside him while the pounding waves buffeted them, throwing them off-balance time and time again. When Jason ran into the tumult he was swept off his feet immediately and lay floundering while a vast wall of water tore its way over him. When he stood up, shivering and gasping, he saw Adam throw the box high into the still mounting sea.

With a savage cry that echoed over the waves, Weston leapt forwards, but it was too late and he aimed a blow to the side of Adam's head, which pitched him forward. Then another mountainous surge of water covered them all.

When Jason surfaced again, he could see Weston swimming – and Adam floating face down on a high ridge of green water.

Jason struck out towards him, grabbed Adam by the hair and

turned him over on his back. At the same moment, Weston surfaced and lunged out at them and missed. The water covered him and then revealed just his craggy face with his long dark hair floating behind him. He looks like a sea-serpent, thought Jason, as he swam on his back, hauling Adam along in a lifesaving position. Weston plunged after them, but suddenly a policeman was there, swimming powerfully and bearing down on all three of them.

Another wave engulfed them while Jason continued to pull Adam towards the beach. Then, suddenly, he felt strong arms on his shoulders and saw a drenched black uniform above him while another policeman, stripped down to shirt and trousers, dashed into the sea towards the struggling Weston. He was followed by another and another – and another.

Jason lay on the beach with Adam beside him. Time had obviously passed but he wasn't sure how much.

One of the policemen was bending down over Adam who was on his face, and his own father was ruffling Jason's hair.

'Weston,' he spluttered.

'They've got him,' said his dad. 'Eileen's confessed everything. Gran found your bed empty and so we called the police. She was worried you'd got too involved. Thank heavens she had more nerve than I had.' He paused. 'There's more to say but I'll tell you later.'

'What do you mean, Dad?' asked Jason blearily.

'It's all OK.'

'You don't—'

'It's all OK. I promise you. We'll talk later.'

'Where's Mum?'

'Here.' Winnie kissed his forehead. 'Adam's going to be fine. He didn't swallow too much water – thanks to you.'

Jason sat up, only to see Weston struggling in the grip of two policemen. Then a tunnel of blackness seemed to come roaring towards him and he didn't know anything more.

Jason soon recovered sufficiently to have a hot bath and go to bed where he slept deeply and dreamlessly. When he woke the sun was streaming through his window and the sky was a deep cobalt blue. A few minutes later, his mother came in.

'How are you feeling?' she asked, sitting gently on the edge of the bed.

'Fine. What about Adam?'

'Still asleep.'

'And his parents?'

'The police say they're helping them with their enquiries – along with that Weston man.'

'Have they got the money?'

'All that was in the drying shed, but five pound notes keep turning up on the beach and under the pier.' She laughed. 'It's like pennies from heaven.' Mum paused. 'Anyway, we've got rid of them at last so Gran's taking over the fortune-telling. She's already insisting on Dad getting a signwriter today to alter "Madame Zorza" to "Vera the Visionary".'

'Supposing Eileen comes back?' asked Jason fearfully.

'She won't,' replied Winnie quietly. 'They're going to be nicked – all three of them. There's no doubt about that.'

'And Adam?' Jason asked hesitantly, just about to build up to what he knew he had to say – and wanted to say.

'Well, he doesn't have any other relations, apparently.' She sighed. 'There's been a bit of a bargain struck.'

'What kind of bargain?'

His mother was silent.

'What is it?' Jason asked anxiously.

'You may not like this.'

'Not like what?' he asked eagerly.

'Eileen asked us to look after Adam for a bit. If the Council try and put him into care, I reckon I can get permission to foster him. She'd be very grateful – she really loves poor old Adam.'

'How long would Adam stay?' asked Jason.

'Until they get out.'

'That might be a long time,' he said.

'I know how you two fight—' she continued doubtfully.

'No we don't,' said Jason.

This time it was his mother's turn to look suspicious.

'What do you mean?'

'I mean, we're mates now. We've been through a lot together.'

'There's something else,' she said.

'Dad?' Jason had been trying not to think about this. 'Are they going to nick him?'

'One of the police said they'd go lenient on him if he really helps them. I don't quite know what "lenient" means, but we can only hope. He's down at the nick now.'

'I'm going down to the beach,' said

Jason. 'I need some time to think.' He paused. 'Is Crab OK?'

She nodded. 'He's fine. I checked him this morning.'

'Thanks, Mum.' He kissed her.

Jason crouched down by the pool and stroked Crab's shell. The September sun gently cosseted his head. Adam stood beside them, looking down, patiently waiting to be drawn in.

'Thanks,' Jason whispered, and Crab's dark eyes stared back at him. Then he looked up at Adam. 'Come and watch him,' said Jason trustingly. 'He's good luck to me. Maybe he'll be the same for you.'

Adam knelt down beside him and said, 'I think we're all going to get along pretty well, don't you?'

'At least we're going to try,' replied Jason cautiously. He stroked the heart shape on Crab's back. 'Wish me luck,' he whispered.

THE END